The FurFins

If you tiptoe to the seashore
and gaze out at the sea,
you might just spot a sparkly tail
or a friendly furry face.
You've just seen a FurFin and found
a very special place.

Shhh, FurFins are real . . .

The FurFins

StarTail and the Sparkly Sleepover

Written by
ALISON RITCHIE

Illustrated by
ALESS BAYLIS

BLOOMSBURY
CHILDREN'S BOOKS
LONDON OXFORD NEW YORK NEW DELHI SYDNEY

Deep beneath the silvery waves,
nestled in a kaleidoscope of colourful coral,
lies the magical Kingdom of Coralia.
This is where the FurFins live.

Look, there's StarTail and her seahorse Shine . . .

StarTail is so excited!
She's invited her friends
for a sleepover.

"Hurray! You're here!" she exclaimed as TinyTail and CherryTail arrived with their seahorses Boo and Yum in tow.

"I've never been to a sleepover before!"
said CherryTail.

"I haven't either," said TinyTail.
"I'm a bit nervous!"

"It's going to be perfect!" said StarTail.
"And it's such a lovely day, why don't
we put up a tent outside?"

Shine, Boo and Yum were so delighted with this idea
that they whizzed round and round in circles
while the FurFins got to work.

It wasn't as easy as they thought and they got in a terrible tangle!

Just then StarTail's new friend RubyTail arrived, with her seahorse Red.
She started laughing when she saw what a pickle they were in.

"Here,
let me help –
I'm good at putting
up tents!"

Soon it was done.

"Teamwork, that's what it takes!" said StarTail,
beaming as she admired the cosy tent. It was decorated
with spring flowers picked by the seahorses.

"I hope Cariad can make it," she added.
"I sent her an invitation yesterday."

Cariad was a great big hug of an octopus, and she always
had a cuddle to spare for the FurFins. The sleepover
would be even better with her there.

Now that they'd put up the tent, the real fun could begin.

First, they needed to organise the feast for later.
CherryTail was in charge. She was famous
throughout Coralia for her
delicious cherry buns.

"We'll all come and help, CherryTail,"
said StarTail.

CherryTail's friends made a terrible mess in her café kitchen,
and RubyTail kept eating the cake mixture – but soon
there was a basket brimming with yummy treats.

They carried it home together, already looking
forward to enjoying the buns that night.

Back at the tent, RubyTail wondered what they should do next.
"I know," said StarTail. "Let's make friendship bracelets
and then we can play a game!"

Soon they each had a colourful bracelet – pink for StarTail,
blue for TinyTail, green for CherryTail
and red for RubyTail.

And none of them could stop laughing when they played musical statues.
They all had to freeze when the music stopped,
but RubyTail just couldn't keep still.

"You'll never win at this!"
chuckled TinyTail.

They were having so much fun that they hardly noticed it getting dark.
It was time for their midnight feast of cupcakes and cherry buns.

"Mmm . . . delicious!"
grinned StarTail.

With warm stomachs, they climbed into their sleeping bags,
excited to be inside their cosy tent.

"This is the best sleepover ever!" grinned RubyTail.

But not everyone was quite as happy . . .

StarTail felt sad that Cariad hadn't come.

"Don't worry, StarTail," said TinyTail.
"I'm sure Cariad will be here next time."

StarTail nodded, feeling better, and soon
they were all yawning and ready for sleep.

It was a dark night and the moon was hidden. The FurFins tossed and turned but none of them could get to sleep.

"Can we turn on the light?" asked TinyTail, who was feeling a bit spooked.

StarTail shuddered. "I can hear something coming!"

Suddenly they saw . . .

...a big SHADOW outside the tent!

The four of them held hands tight.

"What IS that?" whispered RubyTail.

"I don't know!" squealed CherryTail,
"but it's getting CLOSER!"

Just then the tent flap opened . . .

And in came Cariad, carrying armfuls of sparkly fairy lights.

"CARIAD!" squealed StarTail.
"You're here at last!"

"You gave us such a fright!"
said CherryTail.

"I'm so sorry, my lovelies," she said, giving them all a great big octocuddle.
"I wanted you to have these lights for your sleepover.

Not that you need them, of course, because with **friends**
you know you're **never** really in the dark!"

The FurFins snuggled down under the covers and watched the lights twinkle as Cariad read them a bedtime story.

Soon they happily drifted off to sleep.

Before they knew it, the morning sun was shining down.
"Did you sleep well, my lovelies?" yawned Cariad.

They all tucked into a delicious breakfast of cherry buns and chatted
about the night-time surprise, until Cariad said, "It's time for me
to be getting home – but I'll be back to visit soon!"

StarTail gave each of her friends a party bag filled with
treats, and little presents for the seahorses too.

"Thank you, StarTail" said RubyTail.
"I've had so much fun!"

And as the sun rose higher over the coral and the water sparkled,
StarTail looked at the friendship bracelet on her wrist
and smiled at her friends.

"That really was the best
sleepover ever!" she said.

Then, with a flick of their tails, the FurFins

set off together on another exciting adventure.

To the wonderful Pari – A.R.

For Lola – A.B.

BLOOMSBURY CHILDREN'S BOOKS
Bloomsbury Publishing Plc
50 Bedford Square, London, WC1B 3DP, UK
29 Earlsfort Terrace, Dublin 2, Ireland

BLOOMSBURY, BLOOMSBURY CHILDREN'S BOOKS and the Diana logo are trademarks of Bloomsbury Publishing Plc

First published in Great Britain 2022 by Bloomsbury Publishing Plc
Text copyright © Bloomsbury Publishing Plc, 2022
Illustrations copyright © Aless Baylis, 2022

Aless Baylis has asserted her right under the Copyright, Designs and Patents Act, 1988, to be identified as Illustrator of this work

A catalogue record for this book is available from the British Library

ISBN Paperback: 978-1-5266-2407-9
ISBN eBook: 978-1-5266-3058-2

2 4 6 8 10 9 7 5 3 1

Printed and bound in China by Leo Paper Products, Heshan, Guangdong

To find out more about our authors and books visit www.bloomsbury.com and sign up for our newsletters

See you again soon!

The End